ZAC POWER

hardie grant EGMONT

Shock Music
published in 2013 by
Hardie Grant Egmont
Ground Floor, Building 1, 658 Church Street
Richmond, Victoria 3121, Australia
www.hardiegrantegmont.com.au

A CiP record for this title is available from the National Library of Australia.

Cover and Illustrations by Craig Phillips
Cover design by Simon Swingler

Printed in Australia by Griffin Press, an Accredited ISO AS/NZS
14001:2004 Environmental Management System printer.

3 5 7 9 10 8 6 4 2

The paper this book is printed on is certified against the
Forest Stewardship Council® Standards. Griffin Press holds
FSC chain of custody certification SGS-COC-005088. FSC
promotes environmentally responsible, socially beneficial
and economically viable management of the world's forests.

SHOCK MUSIC
BY H.I. LARRY

ILLUSTRATIONS BY CRAIG PHILLIPS

hardie grant EGMONT

CHAPTER 1

There must be a million CDs in this shop! thought Zac Power. *So how do I find the right one?*

Zac was in his local Tunes Super Store. And 'super' was the right word. It was so big you could get lost among the rows of CDs!

Normally, Zac just downloaded his favourite music straight to his SpyPad. But today he wasn't shopping for himself. It was his mum's birthday tomorrow, and she liked music on old-fashioned CDs.

Zac knew what kind of music he liked. The loud, rocking kind from his favourite band, Axe Grinder! But what about his mum? Zac had no idea.

Zac wished his brother Leon had made him a spy gadget that picked out birthday presents. Leon was always making gadgets because he worked for the Tech Division of the Government Investigation Bureau (or GIB for short). Zac also worked for GIB, but he went out on missions.

Zac loved being a spy, but it didn't help with buying presents.

Zac turned a corner and saw a huge stack of boxes. It was a display of red D-Pods, a new music player that he'd seen a few kids using at school.

The D-Pod didn't look that bad, but Zac had seen it up close and he could tell it was a cheap rip-off of the iPod.

Zac knew it would break a week after you bought it. *SO uncool,* he thought, looking closer. *Why would anyone want one?*

But as he looked around, he saw heaps of people wearing red earphones while they browsed. The D-Pod was catching on.

'Excuse me, sir,' said a voice from behind him. It was a Tunes staff member.

'Perhaps your mum would like this CD?'

The man held out a CD. On the cover it said *Twenty Trumpet Classics*.

Zac shrugged. He'd never heard his mum say she liked trumpets before.

Hang on, he thought. *How does this guy know I'm shopping for my mum?* Zac looked closer at the man's name tag. It said:

HELLO. MY NAME IS **GEORGE IAN BOB.**

What a weird name, thought Zac. *Hang on, that spells G-I-B!*

The man winked and said, 'You really should hear this CD, sir. Why don't you listen to it on those headphones over there?' He pointed to a corner of the shop.

Zac took the CD over and popped it in

the player. Then he put the headphones on. Immediately, he felt an itchy tickling in his ears, like something was crawling in.

Ew, thought Zac. *This must be a GIB Wax Scanner!* He tried to keep still as the scanner checked his unique earwax pattern.

Finally he heard a little beep in the headphones. A message came up on the CD player:

ID CONFIRMED.
Welcome, Agent Rock Star!
Ejecting GIB mission disk now.

The CD player opened. Instead of the CD Zac had put in, there was now a shiny little GIB mission disk. Cool!

Zac knew the disk would slot into his

SpyPad, the all-in-one super-gadget that every GIB agent carried. But he couldn't use it in public. He needed to go somewhere private.

Mum's present will have to wait, Zac thought, nodding at the GIB agent and heading for the exit.

But when he crossed into the next aisle, he could barely get through. The aisle was filled with people wearing red D-Pod earphones.

'Excuse me,' Zac said, tapping one of them on the shoulder. It was a teenage girl. 'Can you let me through, please?'

The girl turned around. Her eyes looked a little glazed. 'This D-Pod is so cool,' she said in a robot-like voice. 'You should totally buy one.'

'Yeah,' droned another guy. 'The D-Pod is amazing.'

I don't have time for this, Zac groaned to himself, trying to dodge around the crowds. But people kept shuffling into his path.

Then Zac's spy senses started tingling. *Something's wrong,* he thought. *Everyone who's wearing the D-Pod earphones is acting like a zombie!*

The crowd was now surrounding Zac. They were all shuffling sleepily and mumbling things like, 'D-Pods are awesome.'

Some of them were trying to put the earphones in Zac's ears!

Zac backed up against a huge stack of boxes. *I've got to get out of here!* he thought. *But how?*

CHAPTER 2

Zac felt the boxes digging into his back as the crowd stumbled closer.

There was only one way to go, and that was up!

Luckily Zac had done a lot of karate training in spy school, so he knew how to get out of tight spaces. He took a deep breath, bent his legs and then kicked off the ground with all his might. He leapt into the air and back-flipped over the stack of boxes, landing on the other side. Then he pushed the boxes over, scattering them on the floor.

CRASH!

That should hold the crowd back for a few moments, Zac thought, sprinting for the door as the zombies tried to shuffle over the boxes.

On the street, Zac saw more people wearing D-Pods. They were dragging their feet as they walked, mumbling about how great D-Pods were.

It was kind of creepy, like the old zombie movies Zac had seen on TV.

What is WRONG with them? thought Zac. *Maybe it's something to do with my mission.*

But before Zac could even reach for his SpyPad, he heard screeching wheels.

A moment later, a stretch limo spun around the corner and pulled up next to him. The sun roof rolled open and Leon stuck his head out.

'Zac, what do you think of the D-Pod?' he yelled. 'Tell me, quick!'

'Er – I think it's ugly and creepy,' called Zac. 'Leon, what are you doing here?'

Leon sighed with relief. 'Good, you're not a zombie. Get in!'

Zac pulled open the door and slid into the limo. Inside, there were panels covered in blinking lights, levers and computer displays.

Leon was sitting up one end, surrounded by screws and bits of D-Pods that had been taken apart.

'This is our new CamoSine,' explained Leon, as the limo took off automatically down the street. 'From the outside it looks like a limo, but it's way more useful than that. It's on autopilot at the moment. Have you read your mission yet?'

Zac shook his head. 'But what kind of mission needs a limo?'

Leon gave him a quick grin. 'You'll see in a minute.'

Zac slid the disk into his SpyPad.

CLASSIFIED

MISSION INITIATED: 6 P.M.
CURRENT TIME: 6.30 P.M.

GIB has discovered that the D-Pod, a popular and very cheap music player, is actually a mind-control device. The D-Pod turns its users into 'zombies', who go around convincing other people to buy D-Pods.

GIB suspects that the evil scientist Dr Drastic is behind the D-Pod. Unless a cure can be found in 24 hours, the zombies will be under Dr Drastic's control forever.

YOUR MISSION:

Reverse the zombie mind-control process before it's too late!

~ END ~

Zac looked up at Leon. 'The D-Pod is turning people into zombies? But how?'

Leon looked tense. 'The D-Pod comes with one free song already loaded onto it,' he explained, holding up half a D-Pod. 'The song has a built-in mind-controlling sound pattern called a Zeta wave. When you listen to the song, the Zeta wave sort of fries your brain.'

'And it makes you go around telling other people to buy the D-Pod,' Zac finished.

'That's right,' said Leon. 'The D-Pods are cheap, so everyone's buying one. By this time tomorrow, Drastic could have thousands of people under his control!

But that's not even the worst bit.'

Zac snorted. 'What could be worse than an army of zombies under Drastic's control?'

Leon cleared his throat. 'Er … The mind-control song on the D-Pod is by your favourite band, Axe Grinder.'

Zac's mouth dropped open. 'No way!' he said, horrified.

Leon tapped at his controls and a song began playing inside the CamoSine. 'It's called *Brain Quake*,' he said. 'I've removed the Zeta wave, so it's safe to listen to.'

Zac felt sick, but he forced himself to listen. The song sounded weird. It wasn't like Axe Grinder's other songs at all.

It's almost like they're playing the notes in the wrong order, he thought.

'Terrible,' said Zac when the song had finished. 'OK, so how do we stop Drastic?'

'We go right to the source of the problem,' said Leon. 'And you might feel better once you hear the plan. You're going undercover as a rock star with Axe Grinder!'

CHAPTER 3

Zac almost fell off his seat. 'That is *awesome*!' he yelled.

'I know,' grinned Leon. 'They need a back-up guitarist for their gig at the MegArena tomorrow, so GIB arranged for you to fill in. Rehearsal is in the morning at Lux Hotel in Music City.'

Zac's stomach was flipping with

excitement. 'But Music City is on the other side of the world,' he said. 'We'll never get there in time if we drive a limo.'

Leon smiled. 'True,' he said. 'But the CamoSine isn't a normal limo. Take the wheel and flick those two switches.'

Zac settled into the driver's seat and turned off the autopilot. Next to the first switch was a small label that said 'Flight Mode'.

Zac flicked it, and a second later he saw wide, sleek metal wings sliding out from underneath the limo.

'Cool!' he said, and the CamoSine began picking up speed.

Zac adjusted a few more controls, and

the twin scram-jet engines roared as the limo took off into the air.

WHOOSH!

Lucky we're in a quiet street, thought Zac as they blasted into the sky. *It's not every day you see a flying limo!*

Once the CamoSine had levelled out at 30,000 feet, Zac set the autopilot to head towards Music City. Then he stood up from the controls and turned to face Leon.

'We should get to Music City in about twelve hours,' he said, flopping down on the CamoSine's leather seats. 'So, what kind of disguise kit have you got for me this time? A holographic suit? Nano-particle camouflage masks?'

But Leon shook his head. 'You're going undercover as a rock star,' he said, handing Zac a leather jacket and a pair of sunglasses. 'You just need to look cool! Although you'd better fix your hair – it's all messy.'

Zac rolled his eyes. His hair was *supposed* to look messy. Leon was such a nerd sometimes.

Leon pointed to the sunglasses. 'Those are SHADES, the Secret Highly Advanced Detection and External SpyPad system. You won't be able to use your SpyPad while you're undercover, but you can use these to contact me and GIB. They'll also identify any threats around you.'

'Cool,' said Zac. Then he caught sight of something hidden underneath the seat.

'Is that an electric guitar?' he yelled, jumping down and pulling it out.

It was heaps cooler than Zac's guitar at home – this was a top-model, shiny red Pender Straz. *Awesome!*

Leon rolled his eyes. 'Yes, that's for you too,' he said. 'Don't let it out of your sight. It's been upgraded with high-security features to keep you safe while you're performing. And here's your backpack – there's a few extra gadgets in there you might need.'

The backpack was covered in cool badges and a wicked drawing of a snake, but Zac was heaps more interested in the electric guitar. He couldn't wait to rock out with Axe Grinder on stage!

Leon seemed to guess what he was thinking. 'Don't forget, Zac – you're on a mission. You've got to figure out how to reverse the effect of the D-Pod before it becomes permanent.'

Zac nodded, trying to look serious. Then he remembered something important. 'Leon, what's my rock star identity?'

'Oh, right!' said Leon. 'You're Tom Rocket, wicked guitar player and rocker. GIB have planted a few articles in the newspapers, so everyone will know he's Axe Grinder's new guitarist.'

Zac stood up and peered at himself in the mirror, checking out his leather jacket and making sure his hair looked right. 'Tom Rocket, huh?' he said, grinning. 'I like him already.'

Leon glanced over at the CamoSine's flight deck. Zac had almost forgotten they were still flying through the air.

'We've got hours before we get to Music City,' said Leon. He pulled a little book out of his pocket and held it up. 'Want to do some maths puzzles with me?'

Zac laughed. 'Tom Rocket doesn't do maths puzzles,' he said. 'What else is there to do?'

'Well,' said Leon, 'I suppose there's

this.' He pushed a button, and a huge LCD screen dropped down from the roof of the limo. Two games consoles popped out of the seat cushions. 'It's got pretty much every game ever made on it,' he explained.

Zac grinned. 'Now *that's* more like it.'

CHAPTER 4

It was early morning when the CamoSine's GPS beeped to say they were almost at Music City. Yawning after a night of playing games, Zac slipped into the driver's seat and guided the flying limo down.

They landed in a quiet area outside of town. Zac set the autopilot to head straight for the Lux Hotel, where he was supposed to meet Axe Grinder for rehearsal.

Zac stared out the window as they drove through the city streets. He could see heaps of people wearing the red D-Pod earphones, shuffling along and trying to get other people to buy them too.

Zac shuddered, remembering again that the free song on the D-Pod was by Axe Grinder.

I just can't believe they'd help Drastic to do something so evil, he thought. *There must be a another explanation.*

Zac saw the hotel a long time before they got there. The Lux Hotel was 100 stories tall and shaped like a rocket ship.

It was famous for being very expensive and exclusive. All the big stars stayed there when they toured Music City.

As they got closer to their hotel, the streets became busier and busier until the CamoSine slowed to a crawl. Zac caught sight of a group of people wearing black Axe Grinder T-shirts.

They must be fans here for the gig tonight, he realised. He glanced at his watch. 9 a.m.

We'd better hurry if I'm going to make my rehearsal, he thought. *I don't want to be kicked out of the band before I even play with them!*

Eventually, the CamoSine pulled up outside the Lux Hotel. A long red carpet led up to the hotel's huge revolving door.

The crowds on either side were screaming and waving their hands.

Leon turned to Zac. 'Good luck with your rehearsal,' he said. 'But I, er, forgot to mention one thing. Everyone knows who Tom Rocket is, but no-one knows what he *looks* like. So you'll really have to act like a rock star to get into Lux Hotel.'

Zac winked at him, rock-star style. 'No worries, bro,' he said. He leant over and flicked a switch marked 'External Speaker'. Now everyone outside could hear him.

'Ladies and gentlemen,' said Zac into the microphone in his deepest voice.

The crowd outside went quiet and

everyone turned to stare at the CamoSine.

'He's Axe Grinder's new guitarist,' Zac boomed. 'And he's the hottest new star in rock 'n' roll. You'll all go craaaaazy for … **_TOM ROCKET!_**'

The crowd outside went wild as Zac flung open the door of the CamoSine, slung his guitar over his shoulder and leapt out onto the red carpet.

'Hi, everyone,' Zac yelled, striking a few chords on his guitar. 'Do you want to ROCK?'

The fans cheered even louder.

'I can't hear you!' Zac shouted, strumming his guitar.

Camera flashes were going off all

around him as the crowd roared. *This is so cool*, thought Zac. *They all believe I'm a real rock star!*

But then Zac caught sight of the four security guards standing at the top of the red carpet. They had their arms crossed and they were frowning. Then one of them muttered something to the others.

Zac knew they weren't convinced by his act. He'd have to do something really rock star to get into the Lux Hotel.

The crowd was still cheering for him. 'Play us a song!' someone yelled.

Good idea, thought Zac with a sly grin. He swung his guitar around and set it to AutoAmplify.

'OK, everyone,' he yelled. 'You wanna rock? Let's *rock*!'

Zac slammed down on the guitar. The crowd screamed with excitement as he started playing one of his favourite Axe Grinder songs.

GONNA HAVE TO ROCK YA!
ROCK MY WAY THROUGH!

As Zac played, the fans danced like crazy. He rocked out all the way down the red carpet, high-fiving Axe Grinder fans and finishing off with a wicked solo.

When he finished, he was standing at

the top of the stairs in front of the security guards.

The biggest guard leant forward and looked Zac up and down.

This is it, thought Zac. *If I get past this guy, I'm in. If not ...*

He tried to send out strong 'I'm Tom Rocket' vibes.

The guard seemed to stare at him forever. Then finally he leant back, made a tick on a clipboard, and said, 'Welcome to the Lux Hotel, Mr Rocket. Your band is waiting for you inside.'

Zac gave him a grin, and then strolled through the big revolving door into the Lux Hotel. *I'm in!*

CHAPTER 5

Zac looked around the lobby of the Lux Hotel. *Wow,* he thought. *This place is seriously huge!*

The lobby was the size of a soccer pitch and full of fountains and statues, but the most impressive part was its ceiling.

It didn't *have* one. At least, that was what it looked like. The lobby was open all the way up to the penthouse suite, 100 floors above. It was so high you couldn't even see the top.

There was a reception desk far across the lobby. Zac could see a man in uniform sitting behind it.

'Hi, I'm Tom Rocket,' said Zac, walking over. 'I've got a rehearsal with Axe Grinder.'

'Ballroom number three,' said the receptionist snootily, pointing down a corridor. 'They're filming the rehearsal for a music video, so you'd better hurry.'

Zac's stomach flipped with excitement. *A music video!* He followed the corridor to a set of fancy-looking doors.

There was a sign hanging from the handles:

AXE GRINDER REHEARSAL
– FILMING IN PROGRESS –
NO electronic devices

Zac pushed open the door and was instantly blasted by music coming from inside.

**GOTTA DO IT
GOTTA ROCK THIS HOUSE!**

'Awesome,' Zac said under his breath as he walked inside. The room was as big as the lobby, but crammed full of Axe Grinder fans and cameras and bright lights. And at the far end was Axe Grinder, rocking out on stage!

No wonder they had security guards on the door, thought Zac. *All those fans outside would love to be in here!*

Zac was already late for rehearsal, but how was he supposed to get to the stage? There were people crowd-surfing and diving everywhere. It was a giant mosh pit!

First I should check for any D-Pod zombies, Zac remembered. He tapped his SHADES and set them to Scan.

SCAN MODE ACTIVATED
Zombies detected: 0

That makes sense, thought Zac.

The sign on the door had said 'no electronic devices', so the guards would have stopped anyone wearing earphones.

Now how am I supposed to get through all these people to the stage? thought Zac. He glanced at his watch. It was 10.07 a.m.

No time to waste. Zac opened his backpack to see what gadgets Leon had packed for him. He pulled out a stubby shape with a thick barrel.

A LaserLine! he thought. *Perfect!*

The LaserLine was like a portable grappling hook. It fired a thin, super-strong wire at a target, and then wound it back in. Good for bringing something closer to you, or bringing you closer to something!

Zac adjusted his electric guitar so that it was strapped safely to his back, and then aimed the LaserLine at the stage.

FREEEOOOOOWWW!

The invisible line whirred over the mosh pit and into the wall next to the stage.

THUNK!

It stuck tight. The wire now stretched from Zac all the way across to Axe Grinder.

Now for the quickest way across a mosh pit, thought Zac. *Over the top!*

Still holding the barrel of the LaserLine, Zac ran and took a flying leap onto the dancing moshers.

Then he hit the Retract button on the LaserLine and it quickly wound back,

pulling him towards the stage at top speed.

Everyone cheered as Zac flew over the crowd, waving and pushing him forward with their hands. He wasn't just LaserLining – he was crowd-surfing too!

Just before he got to the stage, Zac let go of the LaserLine and landed with a thump on the stage. Axe Grinder was playing right in front of him. Zac could hardly believe it.

The lead singer, Ricky Blazes, saw Zac and waved him over. 'Hey, you must be Tom Rocket!' he yelled over the music. 'Ready to play?'

Zac grinned and swung his guitar around. 'Am I ever!'

CHAPTER

The band rehearsed for hours, playing every one of their songs all the way through. Zac knew them all and kept up easily, though by the end his fingers were starting to get sore from all the strumming and plucking.

Finally, Ricky Blazes sang the last song and called it quits, motioning for the lights to come on. 'Thanks for coming, guys,' he told the fans. 'The music video will be out next month, so keep an eye out for it. See you tonight at the MegArena!'

Zac stretched as security guards started ushering people out. He felt stiff from hours of playing, but he'd never been so happy in his life!

'That was some pretty radical playing,' said someone from behind him. 'You like our music, Tom Rocket?'

Zac turned around. It was Ricky Blazes.

'Oh, well, you know,' said Zac, trying to be cool. 'I'm a bit of a fan.'

Ricky nodded. 'Thanks, man, that's great. Well, I'd better go get ready in our penthouse suite for tonight's gig. See you later!'

I've got to ask Ricky about the D-Pod, Zac thought as the star turned away. *By the time the gig starts tonight, it'll be too late to stop all those people from being Drastic's zombies forever!*

'Hey, Ricky,' called Zac. 'I was just wondering … What's with that D-Pod song you guys did?'

Ricky turned back to Zac. 'Oh, you mean "Brain Quake"?' he said. 'We just did it for the money. This guy DJ Draz paid us heaps to record this weird song he'd written. It was so bad it'd probably sound better if you played it backwards.'

DJ Draz? thought Zac. *That sounds a lot like Dr Drastic.*

'What does DJ Draz look like?' he asked casually.

Ricky smiled. 'He had this mad white hair and his glass eye kept popping out. That was sort of cool, actually. But he was kind of nasty so we didn't hang with him for long.'

That's Dr Drastic all right! thought Zac.

'Do you know where I could find DJ Draz?' he asked.

'Oh, sure,' said Ricky. 'He's over at –'

'Mr Blazes?' said a voice suddenly.

The security guard from outside had appeared at Ricky's elbow. 'There are some red boxes waiting for you at the front desk. The guy says it's urgent.'

'OK,' said Ricky. 'Listen, Tom, we've gotta go, but it was rad meeting you. I'll catch you at the MegArena!'

Zac sighed as the security guards escorted Ricky and the rest of the band off-stage. He'd had an awesome time playing with Axe Grinder, but he was no closer to solving his mission and saving all those people from being Drastic's zombies.

What do I do now? he thought, checking the time. It was 2.45 p.m. There were just over three hours until the gig started. Then everyone who owned a red D-Pod would turn into a permanent zombie.

Hang on a minute, thought Zac suddenly. *Did that guard say that someone had left RED boxes at reception for Axe Grinder?*

Zac gulped. Maybe they were D-Pods from Drastic!

He sprinted back to where he'd left Axe Grinder, just in time to see the elevator doors closing.

Ricky and the rest of the band were in one of the clear glass elevators. They were all holding red D-Pod boxes in their hands!

Zac groaned. *I've got to catch them before they put those D-Pods in their ears!*

He raced over to the elevator and pressed all the buttons, but nothing happened. Zac knew it would be too late if he didn't find another way to get to Axe Grinder's room.

Zac watched as the elevator started to rise inside the clear glass wall. *I'll just have to beat them to the top,* he thought. *Lucky I'm wearing AeroMasters.*

AeroMasters were one of Leon's new inventions — sneakers that came with built-in pressure suction so that you could walk on any surface. Even up walls!

Zac had never used them before. *These had better work,* he thought grimly.

Zac knelt down and set each shoe to Vertical Mode. Then he took a deep breath and started running up the glass wall.

THWOCK-THWOCK-THWOCK!

Zac's sneakers held tight to the wall as he raced up behind the lift.

THWOCK-THWOCK-THWOCK!

Within seconds he'd almost caught up, but just as he did he caught sight of Ricky Blazes opening the D-Pod box. The other band members were doing the same thing.

THWOCK-THWOCK-THWOCK!

'Stop!' he yelled, but Ricky couldn't hear him.

Zac tried to go faster, but he was too late. Just as he got to the top floor and leapt over the balcony, the elevator door dinged and all the Axe Grinder band members shuffled out wearing red earphones.

'Hey, Tom,' said Ricky Blazes sleepily. 'These D-Pods are rad – and we've got one here for you!'

Oh no! thought Zac. *Axe Grinder have turned into zombies!*

CHAPTER

Zac backed away as the members of Axe Grinder stumbled closer. *This mission is turning into a disaster,* he thought. *What am I going to do now?*

Zac ducked into the penthouse suite. The place was amazing. It had a pool table, guitars everywhere and its own helicopter outside on the helipad.

But there was no time to enjoy it, because Zac could hear Axe Grinder coming in after him. He quickly hid behind a plant.

The band shuffled into the room, mumbling to each other.

'This D-Pod is totally awesome,' Ricky murmured.

'I love my D-Pod,' said the drummer. 'Everyone should have a D-Pod.'

Then Zac heard a familiar voice coming from the next room.

'Is that my favourite band?' said Dr Drastic, walking in with a nasty grin on his face. 'Hello, boys!'

Zac shuddered. He'd met Dr Drastic

heaps of times, but the evil scientist still gave Zac the creeps. He ducked behind another pot plant, trying to stay out of sight.

'Hello, DJ Draz,' murmured the Axe Grinder band members, wandering over to Dr Drastic. 'You should buy a D-Pod. They are amazing.'

Drastic rolled his one good eye. 'I hope my other zombies aren't as dumb as you,' he muttered. 'But at least now you won't keep asking about the Zeta waves I laid over "Brain Quake".'

Zac breathed a quiet sigh of relief. He'd known deep down that his favourite band wouldn't have helped Drastic make something so evil. But he was glad to have it confirmed.

'You were always asking stupid questions,' Drastic was ranting. 'Always making suggestions about how to improve "Brain Quake". The song is an instant classic just the way it is – and it had to be that way to support the Zeta wave.'

The Axe Grinder zombies just stood there.

Suddenly Drastic stopped, and laughed madly. 'But none of that matters now, Axe Grinder!' he grinned. 'I've sent a message to all my zombies to come to your concert tonight. By the time you finish the first song, the effects of the mind-control process will be permanent – and I'll have a whole army of zombies under my control!'

The Axe Grinder zombies watched as Drastic giggled. Zac saw that the drummer was even drooling a little bit.

Drastic sighed happily. 'Now, my zombies, hurry up and get in the chopper. We're going to make our final preparations for the concert tonight. Let's go!'

They're headed for the MegArena early, Zac realised, glancing at the time. It was 4.05 p.m. There were only a couple of hours before the gig! Zac had to get on that chopper with Drastic and the zombies, or else he'd never make it to the MegArena in time.

Zac followed Drastic and Axe Grinder towards the helipad. He made sure he kept well-hidden behind the door until they were all on the chopper.

Can't get in with them, thought Zac, thinking hard as the chopper's blades started spinning. *They'll just turn me into a zombie! But I need to stick with them somehow.*

Then Zac saw the long landing skids on the bottom of the helicopter. *I could hang on under there,* he thought, adjusting the strap of his guitar so that it sat snugly against his back. *But I'll have to time this perfectly!*

The helicopter blades were turning faster and faster, and within moments the chopper had lifted off. Before it could get too high, Zac raced across the helipad and leapt into the air, grabbing hold of the chopper's landing skids.

As the chopper lifted higher, Zac used every muscle in his body to pull himself up to sit on the skids. He held on tight as the chopper picked up speed.

Phew! thought Zac. *Half a second later and I'd be a pancake down on the red carpet!*

The helicopter flew across Music City with Zac hanging on underneath. It was a short flight, but to Zac it felt like forever. Cold wind whipped around his body, and soon he could feel his teeth chattering.

Not long now, he thought, shivering.

Sure enough, the huge MegArena Stadium appeared in the distance a few minutes later.

As the chopper flew closer, Zac could see crowds of people lining up outside. They were shuffling along in a way that was horribly familiar.

His SHADES scanned the crowd.

SCAN MODE ACTIVATED – ALERT! –
Zombies detected: 4000

Zac groaned. He didn't have long before all those people became Drastic zombies forever!

Then he remembered something else. He had get off the chopper before it landed, or he'd be caught and turned into a zombie!

Zac gulped. There was only one way to get off the chopper. And that was straight down ...

CHAPTER 8

Zac stared as the MegArena loomed closer. He'd jumped from great heights before, but usually he had some kind of parachute.

Still shivering from the cold, Zac reached around slowly for his backpack to see what else Leon had given him.

Surely there's something in here I could use

to get down safely, he thought, rummaging as carefully as he could without letting go of the landing skids.

Then Zac pulled out a stretchy rubber outfit. *Oh, sweet!* he thought. *A prototype Human Super-Ball.*

The Human Super-Ball was a loose bag that you put on over your clothes, and when inflated it blew up into a person-sized rubber ball. It was perfect for bouncing from a great height or across long distances.

The only part Zac didn't like was the way you made the Super-Ball deflate again. Leon could only get the rubber to dissolve with human saliva – so if you spat in it, the Super-Ball would turn into a gooey mess within ten seconds. Gross!

But it's my only option, thought Zac, carefully pulling the bag over his clothes without letting go of the chopper.

The chopper was coming in to land, dropping lower and lower.

Zac had to time his jump perfectly.

Closer … a little closer … nearly …

Now!

Zac leapt from the helicopter and pulled the ripcord. Instantly, the Super-Ball puffed out into a see-through rubber cage.

It was weirdly quiet inside as Zac plummeted toward the ground.

The Super-Ball bounced on the foot-path and into the air again. Zac flew over the crowds of people shuffling towards the MegArena.

The ball peaked at about a hundred metres in the air, and then dropped back to the ground again. Zac leant against the clear sides of the ball, trying to guide his next bounce.

BOOOOIIIINNNGGG!

A couple more bounces and Zac was close to the MegArena. From way up high, he could see that the stadium's roof was wide open.

If I do another huge bounce, he thought, *I could probably get right inside the stadium.*

As he dropped to the ground again, Zac slammed his weight downwards, forcing the ball to do an even bigger bounce.

BOOOOIIIINNNGGG!

Zac bounced into the stadium's car park and launched up, up, up – and over the side of the MegArena! Zac flew through the open roof, towards the seats below.

Now the disgusting part, he thought. He sucked up as much spit as he could and spat at the wall of the ball.

Straight away, the rubber started oozing and dissolving until …

SPLAT!

Zac and the suit landed in a big gummy mess inside the stadium. Luckily the combination of rubber and saliva provided a soft landing – even if it was gross.

Ewww! thought Zac, sitting up and pulling bits of dissolved rubber out of his hair. *The things I do for GIB.*

Luckily his guitar didn't have too much gunk on it. Zac wiped it clean and looked around. He'd landed in the seats of the MegArena. He could see the stage far below.

If I'm going to figure out how to reverse the mind-control process, I'd better start there, Zac thought, standing up. He looked at the time. It was 4.50 p.m.

Zac could hear the huge crowd outside the stadium. He knew the zombies were all muttering about how great the D-Pod was.

I've got to hurry, he told himself, running to the stage. He climbed up onto it and started looking around for clues.

The instruments were all set up, but it was dark and quiet. Zac walked around, looking for anything out of the ordinary.

Zac thought back to what Drastic had said at the hotel.

He said they kept trying to improve the 'Brain Quake' song, he remembered, *and that the song had to be the way it was to support the Zeta wave ...*

Zac wandered over to the drum kit, lost in thought. He sat on the stool, recalling something his granny had once told him.

Then Zac had a brainwave. *What if the key to reversing the mind-control is IN the 'Brain Quake' song?* he thought excitedly. *The first time I heard it, I KNEW it sounded wrong!*

But before Zac could do anything else, he heard a faint click. And then –

KER-CHUNK!

A pair of metal bands snapped shut around his waist. The drum kit was booby-trapped!

Then a trap-door opened on the ground in front of him and the drum stool tipped forward.

The metal band around his waist snapped open, dropping Zac underneath the stage!

CHAPTER 9

Zac fell through the trapdoor into a room full of machines and computer screens. A deep, throbbing noise was coming from somewhere below.

Then suddenly Zac realised he'd *stopped* falling entirely. But he hadn't hit the ground. He was now hanging in mid-air!

What is going on? he wondered, looking around.

Zac was in the air about five metres above the ground, surrounded by giant speakers on all sides. That was where the throbbing noise was coming from. The speakers were playing 'Brain Quake'!

'What do you think of my lovely Boom Box?' someone called from below. 'I've created the world's first cage using soundwaves!'

Zac looked down. 'Dr Drastic!' he said, still suspended in mid-air.

'Please,' Drastic called, his glass eye glinting in the light. 'Call me DJ Draz.'

Zac tried to throw himself out of the way of the sound waves, but he was stuck firm.

He wondered how the soundwaves could hold him up if they weren't even that loud. He made a mental note to ask Leon later.

Rats! he thought. *How am I going to get out of this one?*

'I've tied you up so many times, Agent Rock Star,' Dr Drastic said smugly, 'and you always escape. So I thought I'd try something new.'

Zac watched as Drastic walked over to a wall that was covered in controls. There was a giant slider, like the volume control on a stereo.

The slider was currently on three. At the top was eleven, and at the bottom was a big button marked Mute.

'Level three is loud enough to hold you there,' said Dr Drastic, 'but I might try eleven later, just to see what it does to you.'

If I can push that Mute button, I'll be free, thought Zac, his mind racing.

Then Zac realised something else. Even though 'Brain Quake' was playing, he hadn't turned into a zombie!

'Why haven't you added the Zeta wave to your dumb song?' he asked Drastic.

'I'm not stupid enough to play that down here, Rock Star!' said Dr Drastic. 'It would turn me into my own zombie.'

He waved a hand at his controls.

'Anyway, the best part is that all my D-Pods are linked by wireless data sharing, so I can send my zombies new Zeta waves whenever I like.'

Zac wriggled harder, testing the limits of the soundwaves. But all that happened was the collar of his jacket brushed up against his face, and he got a big glob of Super-Ball rubbery gum in his mouth.

Ew ... It tasted disgusting!

Hang on, the gum! Zac realised, holding the glob in his mouth. Maybe he could use it somehow.

He looked over at the Mute button. *It's a long way away,* he thought, *but it's my only chance.* He needed to keep Dr Drastic talking for just one more minute.

'So what are you going to do with all these zombies?' he asked, trying not to choke on the gum.

'Whatever I want!' cried Dr Drastic. 'Once they're mine forever, I could take over a city. No, a country! No, the world!' He leant over the controls, giggling. 'Hmm, what should I do with my next Zeta wave?'

Zac shrugged his shoulders, trying to move his collar into his mouth. He felt another big gloop of rubbery gum there and managed to get it with his tongue.

That should be enough, thought Zac, gagging.

He aimed carefully, and then hocked the gum as hard as he could.

The gum sailed across the room, right in the direction of the Mute button.

SPLATTT!

The gum smacked into the button, and the song cut out instantly. The soundwaves released Zac and he dropped to the floor with an expert roll.

Dr Drastic spun around. 'Agent Rock Star!' he cried.

Zac raced over to the big pile of D-Pods and grabbed one. Before Drastic had time to react, Zac shoved the earphones in his ears!

The D-Pod had an instant effect.

Drastic stood there limply, staring at the ground. 'These D-Pods are totally awesome,' he mumbled. 'Must wear my lovely D-Pod.'

He won't be controlling anyone for a while, thought Zac. *He's become his own zombie!*

CHAPTER 10

Zac had caught Dr Drastic, but it was now 5.47 p.m. There were only 12 minutes until the concert started!

All the zombies would be gathering up in the MegArena, moments away from becoming permanent zombies.

Zac gulped. *Think!* he told himself. *What could reverse the mind-control process?*

Reverse ...

Zac had always thought 'Brain Quake' had its notes out of order. And Ricky Blazes had said it would sound better backwards.

I bet that's it!

There was only enough time to try one thing. Zac hoped desperately that his hunch was right. Otherwise the zombies would be zombies forever.

Zac grabbed his guitar, which was still slung over his back. He ran to the big main door of the lab, but it wouldn't open.

There's no time for me to pick the lock, he thought. *I need to find another way back to the stage.*

He looked up. High above, the trapdoor

he'd fallen through still hung open.

How do I get up there? thought Zac.

His backpack was empty. The Boom Box speakers were too spongy to use his sneakers on. His SHADES and guitar were no good for climbing. All he had left was the cool leather jacket from the CamoSine.

It looked like a normal leather jacket. But since when was anything from GIB normal?

Zac looked closely at it. There were tiny labels sewn all over it that said things like 'laser blow-torch' and 'anti-piranha spray'.

This wasn't a normal jacket. It was a GIB Escape Jacket!

Zac pressed the label marked 'jet packs'.

He grinned as two slim rockets unfolded on his back. Then …

VRRROOOOOMMM!

Zac zoomed up through the trapdoor. He pressed the label again and the jets cut out, plonking him nicely on stage.

The MegArena was now completely full, and Zac's SHADES told him that 90% were D-Pod zombies. But no-one was mumbling anymore.

It was eerily quiet in the huge stadium. Everything was dark … except for a single spotlight at the front of the stage.

Zac had only minutes left.

He walked into the spotlight and swung his electric guitar around, setting it to AutoAmplify. Then Zac took a deep breath and started playing. He started from the end of 'Brain Quake', playing the song entirely in reverse.

At first it was hard to remember the notes, like saying the alphabet backwards. But once he got going, it sounded pretty good.

This isn't a bad song, he thought. *Let's really make it rock!*

He turned the dials on his guitar way up to maximum.

BLAM! ZANG! TWANG!

Zac saw a few of the zombies down the front take off their D-Pods and shake their heads.

It was working! More and more zombies were waking up. Some of them started cheering for Zac. He ran up and down the stage, playing as hard and fast as he could.

TWANNG! *SLAMMM!*

The cheering was getting louder, and some people started dancing.

Then Zac saw the members of Axe Grinder climbing up on stage. They gave him a smile, grabbed their instruments and joined in!

Soon the whole crowd was jumping and cheering.

He'd done it! Everyone was safe! Zac and Axe Grinder hammered down the last notes of the song. A hundred thousand new Tom Rocket fans went wild.

'Nice work, Tom Rocket!' yelled Ricky Blazes. 'Next song is "Rock Your World". You ready?'

Zac was about to say 'You bet!' when a message popped up on his SHADES.

Great work on the mission, Zac! Now, what did you get Mum for her birthday? From Agent Tool Belt (Dad) x

~ MISSION CHECKLIST ~
How many have you read?

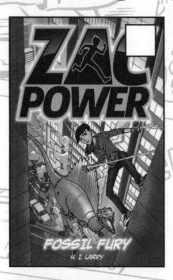

FOSSIL FURY
H. I. LARRY

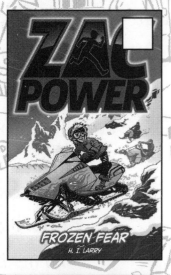

FROZEN FEAR
H. I. LARRY

SHOCK MUSIC
H. I. LARRY

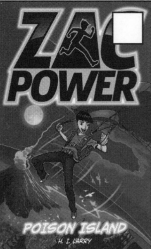

POISON ISLAND
H. I. LARRY